Number Ten

Dorling Kinderlsey
www.dk.com

Editor Fiona Munro
Designer Lisa Hollis

Published in Great Britain in 1997
by Dorling Kindersley Limited, 9 Henrietta St, London WC2E 8PS
This edition published in 2000

A CIP catalogue record for this book is available from the British Library.

ISBN 0-7513-6710-9

Color reproduction by DOT Gradations
Printed in Hong Kong by Wing King Tong

Number Ten

COLIN AND JACQUI HAWKINS

Dorling Kindersley

"Double trouble, that's me!" said Number Ten.

Number Ten lived in the oddest house in Numbertown. It was an old windmill with ten broken windows.
The address was 10, Number Lane.
It was the tenth house in Numbertown.
"It's very tatty," said scatty Number Ten.

Inside the old windmill, Number Ten had ten buckets to catch the water from ten leaks in the roof.

Drip! Drip! Drip! Drip! Drip! Drip! Drip! Drip! Drip! Drip!

Ten buckets for ten drips!

At night it was so cold, Number Ten
needed ten hot water bottles to keep warm.

Brrrrrrrrr!

Off to slumber,
sleepy Number.

Every day, Number Ten danced ten times to the top ten records.

He never went to bed before the Numbertown clock struck ten.

Bong! Bong! Bong! Bong! Bong! Bong! Bong! Bong! Bong! Bong!

All the other Numberlies were fed up
with Number Ten's house.
Not only was the windmill old and tatty,
but it was also very noisy.

Creak! Groan!

Often it kept everyone awake, especially
Number Nine who lived next door.
"What a noisy nightmare!" he moaned.

One night, there was a terrible storm.
The wind howled and the rain lashed down.
Ten flashes of lightning flashed and
ten rolls of thunder
rumbled.

Crack!
Thunder!
Rumble!

"This is a force ten gale warning,"
crackled the radio.

"Out at sea is no place to be!"

shivered Number Ten.

Suddenly, there were ten loud knocks at the door.

Knock! Knock! Knock! Knock! Knock! Knock! Knock! Knock! Knock! Knock!

"Who's there?" asked Number Ten.
It was a very wet Number Six.
"Number Nine is still out at sea," he gasped,
"and the light in the lighthouse has gone
out and . . . he'll never find his way home!"

"Oh no!" cried Number Ten.

Then Number Ten had a brilliant idea!

"It might just work!"

Let's hurry !

Number Ten
rushed upstairs,
found ten torches
and tied them onto the
ten sails of the windmill.
"That should lighten things up a bit!"
said Number Ten.

"Let's make it bright,
this stormy night!"

Whizzzzzzzzz!

The sails on the
windmill whirled
round and round.
The ten torches
shone out brightly
into the dark,
wet, windy night.

"It's like a giant firework!" said Number Ten,
beaming with delight. "Number Nine is
sure to find his way home now!"

"That's amazing, you **are** clever!"
shouted all the other Numberlies.

Far out across the dark sea, Number Nine saw the bright light and sailed towards it.

Ten minutes later, he arrived home safely. Number Nine thanked Number Ten at least ten times. He was very pleased to be home.

"Hurrah for Number Ten!"

cheered all the Numberlies.

The Numberlies were so pleased with Number Ten that they all helped repair the old windmill. They mended ten windows, scrubbed ten floors and patched ten holes. Then they painted the windmill bright blue and the ten sails a sunny yellow!

"This is the best home in Numbertown. I'll give it ten out of ten!"

said Number Ten.

All the Numberlies cheered!